I AM

No Nits!

JANE CLARKE

Illustrated by
JAN LEWIS

KINGFISHER
An imprint of Kingfisher Publications Plc
New Penderel House, 283-288 High Holborn
London WC1V 7HZ
www.kingfisherpub.com

First published by Kingfisher 2006
This edition published by Kingfisher 2007
2 4 6 8 10 9 7 5 3 1

A CIP catalogue record for this book is available from the British Library.

ISBN 978 0 7534 1552 8

Printed in China
1TR/0507/WKT/(CG)/115MA

Contents

Chapter One

In the peaceful Kingdom of Hairia, everyone was busy growing their hair. Princess Primrose rushed into the Palace. She pushed her long, long hair out of her eyes.

"Daddy!" she squeaked. "It's in the newspaper! There are nits in the Kingdom of Hairia!"

"There are nits in every kingdom, Princess," said the King, strumming his guitar.

"Not that sort of nits! The sort of nits that hatch into itchy head lice!" Princess Primrose told him. "I might catch them! You might catch them too!"

The King pushed his long hair out of his eyes. "Itchy nits here, itchy nits there, get those head lice out of my hair," he sang.

"Stop singing and do something, Daddy!" Primrose said.

The King took off his dark glasses and
put down his guitar.
"No problem, Princess," he said.

The King went out onto the balcony of the palace. The crowd below looked like a sea of hair. Two or three people were scratching their heads.

The King spoke into the microphone. "Everyone must wash their hair!" he announced. "No nits in the Kingdom of Hairia!"

The crowd gulped. No one in Hairia liked washing their long, long hair.

Chapter Two

Ouch! Ouch! Ouch!

For days, the Kingdom of Hairia rang with cries of "Ouch!" as shampoo got in everyone's eyes. The sky over Hairia was full of bubbles. But it was no good.

"Head lice like clean hair!" Princess Primrose said. "The nits are spreading."

The King strummed his guitar.
"It's not a dream, nits like it clean,"
he sang.
"Stop singing!" Princess Primrose
wailed. "I might catch them. You
might catch them! Do something,
Daddy!"
"No problem, Princess," said the King.

The King went out onto the balcony of the Palace. The crowd below looked like a sea of hair and hands. Half of the people were scratching.

The King took the microphone in one hand and held up a hairbrush in his other hand.

"This is the only hairbrush in the Kingdom of Hairia!" he announced. "Everyone must brush their hair with it! No nits in the Kingdom of Hairia!"

The crowd muttered. No one in Hairia ever brushed their hair.

Oww! Owww!

Owwwww!

For days, the Kingdom of Hairia rang with cries of "Owww!" as people dragged the hairbrush through their hair. But it was no good.

"Head lice like people to share a hairbrush!" Princess Primrose said. "The nits are spreading!"

"Never share when you brush your hair," sang the King, strumming his guitar.

"I might catch them! You might catch them!" Princess Primrose cried. "Stop singing and do something, Daddy!"

"No problem, Princess," said the King.

Chapter Three

From the balcony of the Palace, the crowd below looked like a field of fidgety fingers. Everyone was scratching. The King spoke into the microphone. "No more scratching!" he announced.

“Everyone must cut their hair!”

The crowd gasped.

No one in Hairia ever cut their hair.

The gasp
turned into a
mumble,

the mumble
turned into
a mutter,

and the
mutter
turned into
a roar.

"Do something, Daddy!" Princess Primrose yelled.

"No problem, Princess," said the King. "Send for the scissors!"

The King cut his hair right there and then and called for his guitar.

"No nits today, my hair has gone away," he sang.

"Cool!" gasped the crowd.

For days, the Kingdom of Hairia rang with cries of "Cool!" as the people cut their hair. The streets of Hairia were ankle-deep in hair.

"No Nits Today" reached number one in the charts.

"No Scratching" signs went up everywhere.

"That's it!" said the King at last.
"There are no more nits in Hairia."
"Phew!" said Princess Primrose,
combing her long, long hair. "Thank
goodness I didn't catch head lice."
But nits take a while to hatch…

Chapter Four

The King and the Princess went out onto the balcony of the Palace. The crowd below were admiring each other's new haircuts. The royal trumpeters trumpeted. There was a roll of drums.

The King took the microphone.

"There are no nits in the Kingdom of Hairia!" he announced.

"Hooray!" cheered the crowd.

The King strummed his guitar.

Everyone joined in singing "No Nits Today". "No more scratching, scratching's catching," they sang.

At that very moment, Princess Primrose felt something. Something moved in her long, long hair. Something itchy.

She scratched her head.

The crowd stopped singing.

Princess Primrose carried on scratching her head.

"No more scratching, scratching's catching!" the crowd chorused, scratching their heads.

"She's got nits!" someone screeched.

"Nits! Nits! Nits!" the crowd roared.

"Do something, Daddy!" shrieked Princess Primrose.

The King checked out Primrose's head.

“Your hair’s crawling with head lice, and there are lots of nits waiting to hatch!” he whispered.

“Off with her hair! Off with her hair! Off with her hair!” chanted the crowd.

“This is a problem, Princess,” said the King.

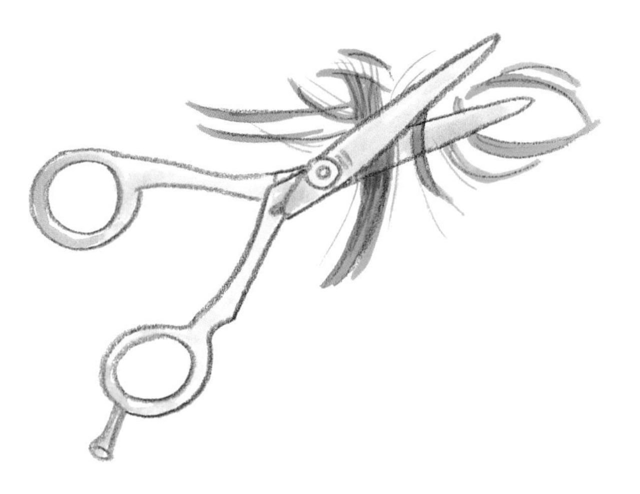

Chapter Five

"Off with her hair!" the crowd shouted over and over again.

"Send for the scissors," said the King.

Princess Primrose shut her eyes.

"I wish I didn't have nits!" she wept. "I wish I could keep my long, long hair!"

Pffffff!

A very hairy fairy with a moustache and beard appeared in a puff of smoke.

"Wow!" gasped the crowd.

"Who are you?" sniffled the Princess.

"I am your Hairy Godmother," said the hairy fairy. "I shall grant your wish."

Princess Primrose's Hairy Godmother waved her wand. A comb flew into her hand.

"Nits are no problem!" she said. "You can keep your long, long hair. Just wash it, condition it, and comb it again and again and again with this special comb."

She twirled her wand once more. A bottle flew into her hand.

"Or use this bottle of special shampoo, and comb your hair with the special comb again..."

"...and again and again?" asked Princess Primrose.

"That's right!" said the Hairy Godmother, twirling her moustache. "And don't share brushes, combs or hats!"

Pffffff!

She disappeared in another puff of smoke.

Chapter Six

The King put on his dark glasses and spoke into the microphone.

"Now we know what to do if we get nits, we can grow our hair long again!" he announced.

He strummed his guitar. “Nits aren’t our problem anymore, let’s grow our hair down to the floor!” he sang.

The crowd went wild.

Princess Primrose scratched her head. “I have the longest hair in Hairia,” she said. “All that combing again and again and again is far too much trouble. Stop singing and do something, Daddy!”

The King took out the scissors,
shampoo and comb.
"No problem, Princess," he said.

The King sent for a mirror so that Princess Primrose could see her short, spiky hair.

“It’s great!” Primrose said. “From now on, I shall have the shortest hair in Hairia! Thank you, Daddy!”

“No problem, Princess,” said the King.

So Princess Primrose kept her hair short, while the King and all the people of Hairia grew their hair long again.

And they all lived happily ever after, as you'd expect from a hairy story... unless you happen to be a nit, of course!

About the Author and Illustrator

Jane Clarke has been an archaeologist, a teacher and a library assistant, but she likes being a writer best of all. She started to make up stories when her sons were small, but she didn't write anything down until they were big and hairy. Since then, she's been itching to write a hairy story.

Jan Lewis lives in the south of England with her two large sons and two small dogs. Sometimes her hair does very strange things in the mornings but luckily she has never had nits. Her two sons did when they were little, though, so Jan knows all about combs and conditioners.

Tips for Beginner Readers

1. Think about the cover and the title of the book. What do you think it will be about? While you are reading, think about what might happen next and why.

2. As you read, ask yourself if what you're reading makes sense. If it doesn't, try rereading or look at the pictures for clues.

3. If there is a word that you do not know, look carefully at the letters, sounds, and word parts that you do know. Blend the sounds to read the word. Is this a word you know? Does it make sense in the sentence?

4. Think about the characters, where the story takes place, and the problems the characters in the story faced. What are the important ideas in the beginning, middle and end of the story?

5. Ask yourself questions like:

Did you like the story?
Why or why not?
How did the author make it fun to read?
How well did you understand it?

Maybe you can understand the story better if you read it again!